_____'s

Jungle Book

Published by Scholastic Inc., 90 Old Sherman Turnpike,
Danbury, Connecticut 06816.

0-7172-7832-8

Printed in the U.S.A.
First printing, March 2005

WALT DISNEY

THE JUNGLE BOOK

SCHOLASTIC INC.

New York Toronto London Auckland Sydney
Mexico City New Delhi Hong Kong Buenos Aires

Deep in the Indian jungle, Bagheera the panther heard a strange sound. He discovered that it was a Man-cub! The baby boy was in a basket, which lay in a half-sunken boat on the river.

6

Bagheera felt sorry for the baby. He carefully carried the basket ashore.

"The Man-cub will never survive without a mother," Bagheera said to himself. Then he remembered that a wolf family lived nearby. Perhaps they would adopt the Man-cub.

Bagheera brought the basket to the wolves' den. When Akela, the mother wolf, and her cubs found the laughing baby, they smiled. Rama, the father wolf, was not so pleased at first. But soon he, too, was smiling at the Man-cub.

The wolves named the Man-cub "Mowgli." For 10 years, he lived happily in the jungle. Mowgli learned many things from the wolves: how to scratch himself . . .

. . . how to play dead . . .

. . . and how to run!

But one day, there was some terrible news in the jungle. Shere Khan the tiger had returned. The fearsome tiger hated all humans because a hunter had once shot at him. So Mowgli was in danger!

Late that night, the wolf pack gathered with Bagheera on Council Rock. They decided that Mowgli must leave. Bagheera knew of a Man-village, where he could take Mowgli and he would be safe.

But taking Mowgli to the Man-village would not be easy. "This is my home," protested Mowgli, as Bagheera tried to pry him from a tree. "I don't want to leave the jungle!"

Reluctantly, Mowgli began
the journey to the Man-village
with Bagheera.

Night began to fall. When
they came to a big tree,
Bagheera decided they would
spend the night there. Bagheera
gave the boy a lift up.

"Go to sleep," Bagheera told Mowgli,
as they settled themselves on a branch.

But they were not alone. Kaa the snake
was hiding in the tree. He thought Mowgli
would make a tasty treat!

"Yes, Man-cub," Kaa whispered, as he
slithered down the tree,
"go to sssleep."

Mowgli woke up and saw Kaa. "Leave me alone,"
he said to the snake.

"Do not be afraid, Man-cub," said Kaa. "Trussst
me. Go to sssleep."

Kaa stared at Mowgli. Mowgli began to feel dizzy.
He was under Kaa's spell. Kaa wrapped his long tail
around Mowgli.

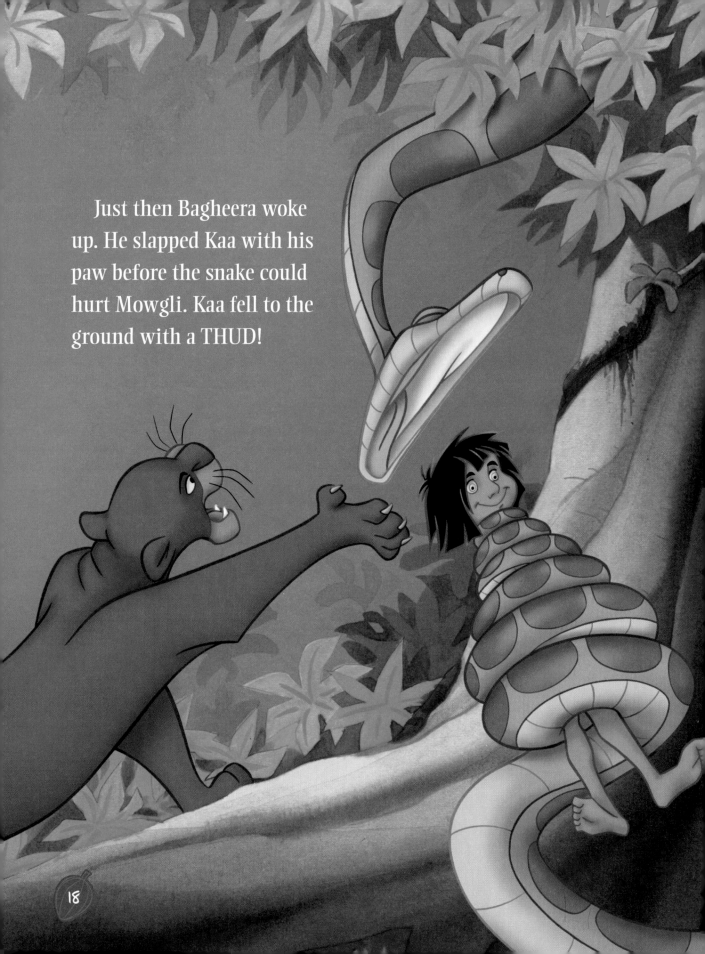

Just then Bagheera woke up. He slapped Kaa with his paw before the snake could hurt Mowgli. Kaa fell to the ground with a THUD!

18

"You have made
a ssserious
missstake, Bagheera," said
Kaa, as he slithered off.

Bagheera told Mowgli,
"You see, the jungle is too dangerous
for you. You belong in the Man-village.
We will go there in the morning."

But Mowgli still did not want to live in the Man-village. So he left early the next morning.

"I can take care of myself!" Mowgli said to Bagheera, as he walked away. "I don't need anyone."

But after a while, he felt very lonely.

Then Mowgli heard somebody singing.
It was Baloo—a big, friendly bear.
"Well, hello there, Little Britches,"
Baloo said to Mowgli, with a smile.
They quickly became friends.

21

Baloo taught Mowgli how to
dance like a bear . . .
and growl like bear . . .

. . . and even how to
fight like a bear!

"I want to stay in the jungle
with you, Baloo!" said Mowgli.

23

"I like being a bear," Mowgli told Baloo,
as they floated down the river.
Neither of them noticed that several
monkeys were watching them . . .

Before Baloo could stop them,
the monkeys grabbed Mowgli!
They brought Mowgli to their
leader, King Louie.

"So you're the Man-cub,"
said King Louie. "Crazy!"
"I'm not crazy. You are!"
said Mowgli.

"Have some bananas," said King Louie, shoving two into Mowgli's mouth. King Louie struck a deal so that Mowgli could stay in the jungle. Then the monkeys decided to celebrate. Everybody started dancing.

Meanwhile, Baloo found the ancient
ruins where the monkeys lived. In order to
rescue Mowgli, Baloo disguised himself as a
big monkey and danced right into the party.

Baloo's plan worked! While the monkeys sang
and danced, he carried Mowgli out of the ruins.

"Thanks for rescuing me," said Mowgli. "I didn't want to be a monkey. I would rather be a bear, like you."

"But you are not a bear," Baloo said sadly. "The jungle is too dangerous for you. You belong in the Man-village."

"You are just like Bagheera!" shouted Mowgli. "I don't want to go to the Man-village! I can take care of myself!"

So Mowgli ran away
from Baloo, too.

Mowgli ran through the jungle. Then he ran right into Shere Khan!

"Do you know who I am, Man-cub?" asked Shere Khan.
"Yes. But I am not afraid of you," said Mowgli.

"Everyone is afraid of me," Shere Khan said smugly. "Well you don't scare me," said Mowgli.

"Ah, you have spirit for one so small," said the tiger. "You deserve a sporting chance. I will close my eyes and count to 10. It makes the chase more interesting."

Shere Khan began to count. But Mowgli didn't run away.
He wasn't about to be bullied by the tiger.

This only angered Shere Khan. Just as he lunged
for Mowgli, Baloo came to the rescue! He grabbed
the tiger's tail to try to save the Man-cub.

Suddenly a bolt of
lightning flashed in the
sky. The lightning hit a
nearby tree, starting a fire.

37

Mowgli picked up
a burning branch and
tied it to Shere
Khan's tail. There
was only one thing
Shere Khan feared:

FIRE.

He let out a roar and fled.

Bagheera and Baloo
were so happy to see that
Mowgli was not hurt!

"We're glad you're safe, Little Britches," said Baloo, when Mowgli ran up to the big bear and gave him a big hug.
Mowgli hugged Bagheera, too. He was happy to see his friends.

It was beginning to get
dark, so they found a safe
place to rest. Soon they
were all fast asleep.

The following morning, the three friends walked to the river. Mowgli was explaining to Baloo and Bagheera how he could stay in the jungle—especially now that Shere Khan had gone away.

When they arrived at the river, they heard someone singing. They crept closer and saw a young girl fetching some water from the river.
"What's that?" asked Mowgli.
"That is a Girl-cub," Bagheera told him.

Mowgli had never seen a Girl-cub. He decided to take a
closer look. She turned and saw him. She smiled at Mowgli and
dropped her jug of water.
"Hey, she did that on
purpose!" Baloo said,
watching from the bushes.
"Quite right," said
the wise panther,
with a smile.
Mowgli quickly
picked up the jug
the young girl
had dropped and
refilled it
with water.
Then he waved
good-bye to his friends and followed her into the Man-village.

"Well, Baloo, Mowgli will live in the Man-village from now on," said Bagheera, as they headed back into the jungle. "We will miss him, but he is where he belongs."

"Yes," agreed Baloo, "but I still think he would have made one swell bear!"

The End

Here's some jungle fun!

Look back in the story and try to find these wild pictures.